Read more  books!

Llama Drama

It's Showtime!

Rose Impey

Illustrated by Ali Pye

HarperCollins *Children's Books*

First published in Great Britain by HarperCollins *Children's Books* 2013
HarperCollins *Children's Books* is a division of HarperCollins*Publishers* Ltd,
77-85 Fulham Palace Road, Hammersmith, London W6 8JB

The HarperCollins website address is: www.harpercollins.co.uk

1

Text copyright © Rose Impey 2013
Illustrations copyright © Ali Pye 2013

ISBN 978-0-00-749478-1

Rose Impey and Ali Pye assert the moral right to be identified as the
author and illustrator of this work.

Printed and bound in England by Clays Ltd, St Ives plc

My good friend, Shoo

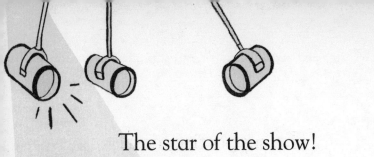

The star of the show!

The supporting cast!

Chapter One

Meet the Llamas

Farmer Palmer's llamas were famous throughout the whole state of Texas, and beyond. Year after year they won the top prizes at the County Fair. When people asked him, "What's your secret?" Farmer Palmer always replied, "It's pretty simple:

my llamas are well bred and they're well fed. And I sure am proud of 'em."

But he wasn't half as proud as Mama Llama.

Back at the farm, Mama Llama gazed fondly around the field at her large llama family. She stretched her long neck and twitched her nose with pleasure as she watched her two eldest sons, Leo and Lamar, neck-wrestling again.

"Those boys," she said proudly to Papa Llama. "Always fighting."

"Oh, yes," Papa Llama agreed. "Llamas will be llamas."

Especially the boys, he might have added. Especially now that Farmer Palmer

was about to choose the best and bravest
llama to guard his – also prize-winning –
flock of sheep, Leo and Lamar were even
more determined to prove themselves.

Of all their many children, Papa Llama thought those two were the finest examples. Everything a llama should be: loud, proud and intensely competitive. All the howling and yelping they were doing now was a sure sign those boys meant business.

Leo *the Lionheart*, as his mother liked to call him, was their eldest. He was a big, brave, dark brown llama and a born leader. At least, that's what Leo often told himself.

Lamar was piebald grey, and even more handsome. As second eldest, Lamar had always stood in his brother's shadow. But one of these days he was going to beat Leo and today might just be the day. After all, he was nearly as tall, with slightly longer legs – excellent for kicking. He was putting them to good use right now, trying to knock Leo off balance. As he lashed out, Lamar yelped loudly. If he was going to win, he wanted to make sure everyone in the field was watching.

But it was Leo who took Lamar by surprise, suddenly ramming him with his chest. Lamar didn't see that coming.

"Oofff!" he groaned as

all the air burst out of him. He stepped back for a moment, slightly winded.

Their sister, Latisha, was standing nearby, watching the boys' moves.

"Ram him back!" she yelled at Lamar. "Don't just stand there like a stunned sheep."

"Who are you calling a sheep?" Lamar yelled back.

"You, you big woolly jumper," she replied.

And just then, while Lamar was still arguing with his sister, Leo aimed a huge jet of spit in his brother's direction. It landed smack on top of Lamar's head, completely flattening his carefully arranged hairstyle.

"*Now look what you did!*" Lamar yelled.

"And after I just washed it!" Leo might be bigger, but Lamar was much more vain. "It wasn't fair; I wasn't even looking!"

But Leo was gone, already doing a lap of honour round the perimeter of the field.

"Who's the greatest? I'm the greatest," he chanted to himself as he trotted. *"Who's the loser? Lamar's the loser!"*

Leo lost no time in reminding everyone that he was still *Top Llama*. There was no doubt in his mind now that tomorrow Farmer Palmer would choose him to guard his sheep.

Oh, boy! Leo thanked his lucky stars he hadn't been born a sheep. Sheep were so stupid and so jittery. Born cowards, in his opinion; sitting targets for any wily wolf or passing prairie dog – or cunning coyote. But that was why they needed a brave and strong llama to guard them – a llama like him.

Hanging out with a flock of silly sheep wasn't exactly Leo's idea of fun. But everyone knew it was the *Top Job* so, obviously, it had his name on it.

"I'll soon lick them into shape," he told himself. "I'll bang a few woolly heads together, if I have to. They'll quickly learn who's boss."

"*Who's the greatest? I'm the greatest,*" Leo chanted again.

Lamar watched his brother showing off

and it made him spitting mad. "That was all your fault," he snapped at his sister, determined to blame someone. "If you hadn't come butting in, I would have—"

"What? What would you have done?" Latisha snapped back. "You're useless and you know it. Even I could beat you. Come on, you wanna try?"

Huh! Lamar could easily beat his sister. She was only a girl, after all, and younger than him by a couple of seasons. But *if* she were to win – oh, man, he would never hold his neck up high again. Even he had to admit, Latisha was one tough llama. It was possible, in a couple of years, that she might even beat her brothers and, oh, what a terrible day that would be!

No, Lamar couldn't take that kind of risk. So he pretended he hadn't heard his sister's challenge and moved off, looking for a nearby fence post. He rubbed his head against it to clear the spit from his topknot and try to smarten himself up. Lamar might not have beaten Leo *today*, but he could still be the farmer's new Guard Llama. After all, size wasn't everything. He was more athletic than Leo. He had the legs. And looks were important too. Lamar had a much finer profile. Wasn't that why Mama Llama had given him his second name: Lincoln?

"After the president, Abraham Lincoln," she told him. "So distinguished."

Lamar rubbed his topknot until it was standing tall, then he shook it so it fell over his eyes. A pretty cool look, in his opinion. Tomorrow, if he impressed Farmer Palmer, he could still turn out to be the winner.

Lamar trotted down to a corner of the field where his youngest sisters – and some of their attractive friends – hung out. *Who cares about Leo?* he asked himself, *I'm certainly the girls' favourite.*

The young llamas crowded round him, batting their eyelashes and giggling. Lamar gave them a friendly nudge and a wink. Oh, yes, he had a way with females. *When I'm Guard Llama,* he thought, *I'll have that flock of silly sheep following me around. Just watch me.*

"Tchhh," Latisha tutted to herself and tossed her head. "Honestly!"

What a poser her brother was. And what an idiot. She could have neck-wrestled

Lamar to the ground, no problem! Maybe not Leo yet, but give her a year or two... Her brothers didn't impress her one little bit. But then Latisha had something neither of them had: an active brain.

There was no good reason why *she* shouldn't be Farmer Palmer's Guard Llama. *Where did it say it couldn't be a girl?* she'd asked Mama Llama. Life was so unfair.

If Latisha were in charge of the llama world, things would run very differently. She would lay down some rules of her own... *No spitting*, for a start. It just wasn't necessary in her view. The way Leo had done it so sneakily too, just when Lamar wasn't looking.

Instead, there would be properly organised contests, real tests of strength and endurance. After that, the winner would have to take an intelligence test, which would rule out most of her family. Oh, they all liked to think they were clever, but none of them were in Latisha's league.

But even Latisha had to admit that, compared to sheep, llamas were like the Einsteins of the animal world. In her opinion, sheep were *really* dumb. D-U-M-B, dumb. Dumb as...

Hmmm, now she thought more about it, Latisha had to ask herself, *why*? Why would anyone want to leave their own herd, to hang out with those woolly-brained mutts?

All alone too! Llamas were social animals. They weren't meant for a solitary life. No, she didn't really want the job – *she just wanted to beat her brothers*!

Latisha looked for a quiet corner to make her plan, where she wouldn't be distracted by the sight of that big-headed brother, Leo, still puffing himself up and acting like he'd already won. Or that idiot, Lamar, and his even more idiotic fan club.

"Tchhh," she tutted again. Oh, why couldn't they all be more like her? Latisha wondered.

Later that evening, when the family gathered together, Mama and Papa

Llama nuzzled each other fondly. They congratulated themselves yet again on what a good job they'd done with their children.

Tomorrow was a big day for all of them. Whichever one Farmer Palmer chose – Leo, Lamar, or even Latisha – Mama and Papa Llama would be happy. They were glad to see that, for now at least, the three young llamas appeared to have put aside their quarrels. They were discussing what it might really mean, if they did get chosen.

"It'd mean leaving the family *forever*," Lamar pointed out a little nervously.

"Just to babysit a load of brainless

sheep," grumbled Leo.

"Having to fight off any crafty coyotes out there, *all on your own!*" Latisha added.

But this thought again stirred up her brothers' competitiveness.

"Pfff," Leo huffed. "I feel sorry for any coyote crazy enough to come sniffing around *my* flock of sheep," he bragged.

"Just one crazy coyote?" Lamar scoffed. "A whole pack of coyotes could attack *my* flock and they'd still be able to sleep like babies."

"One llama? Against a whole pack!" said Latisha dismissively. "Tchhh! What planet are you on, brother? You'd need a plan, a strategy and, let's face it, I'm the only one with the brains to deliver that."

The llamas were soon bickering again, until their attention was drawn to a small crowd that had gathered round their other brother, Lewie, the next oldest male llama in the family. Lewie was showing off again!

"Oh, boy," sniffed Leo.

"What an embarrassment," hissed Lamar.

"Tchhh," tutted Latisha.

Suddenly, the three were united once more. If there was one thing they could absolutely agree on it was this – tomorrow, when Farmer Palmer came to choose his new Guard Llama, the one he would *definitely* not be choosing was Loopy Lewie!

Chapter Two

Meet the Star of the Show

Lewie was performing – again. He could never resist playing to the crowd. There was nothing he liked better than to be surrounded by a sea of adoring faces. The young llama had just run through some of his circus tricks – his juggling was always a crowd pleaser. Now, by popular demand, he was doing his famous impressions. He stuck out his chest, swung his bottom from side to side and asked, "Who's this?"

"Farmer Palmer!" everyone cried out, easily recognising the farmer's waddling walk. Next he did the farmer's kind but fussy wife, with her bobbing head and fast footsteps. Then their cute little daughter, Millie, skipping along, humming to herself... The llamas stamped their feet in appreciation, especially Liberty, Lewie's twin sister. She was Lewie's biggest fan.

"OK, who's this?" Lewie asked, before launching into another instantly recognisable impression. This time he imitated his swaggering brother, puffing himself up and chanting, "*Who's the greatest?*"

"Leo!" everyone shouted and cheered.

"And this?"

"Lamar!" They screamed with laughter when Lewie shook his topknot, pretending to be *oh, so cool.*

Even Latisha laughed... well... brayed actually. She always enjoyed seeing Lamar embarrassed. But she soon stopped laughing.

"How about this?" Lewie asked next. He shook his head and stuck his nose in the air, all the while tutting, "Tchhh! Tchhh! Tchhh! Honestly!"

"Latisha!" The llamas almost cried with laughter. They started copying Lewie's impression, tutting at each other, their noses in the air.

"Not so funny now?" Lamar asked, enjoying the sight of his sister's red face.

"More! More!" the llamas cried.

But Lewie quickly moved on to something new. He'd been practising and was keen to try it out on an audience.

"Watch this, everyone!" he said. "Watch me die."

Lewie went into a long, slow, lingering death scene, where he pretended to have been shot. He began with a high, piercing scream and clutched his heart. Then, moaning and groaning, he fell on to his back legs... then his front legs gave way and he rolled heavily on to the ground. Just when everyone thought he'd completely expired, Lewie suddenly dragged himself to his feet. He staggered a few steps, still groaning, before crashing magnificently to the ground once more – lifeless at last.

Mama Llama gasped, convinced he must have broken every bone in his body. The other llamas held their breath. One or two of the younger ones genuinely thought he'd died and began to cry. So the surprise was even greater when Lewie leapt to his feet, totally unharmed, and shouted "Ta-daa!" before taking several bows.

"More! More! More!" the llamas brayed.

Mama Llama stamped her feet in appreciation too, but Papa Llama just shook his head, not exactly in despair, but something like it. He'd never known what to make of Lewie. The boy was a total mystery to his father.

Leo, Lamar and Latisha didn't share their mama's admiration either. They thought Lewie was a *dis-as-ter*. They'd always made fun of him, calling him Loopy Lewie and Lewie the Loser and, in Latisha's case, Drama Llama. Not to mention other, even meaner, names at times.

Lewie was used to them ganging up on him. And he would be the first to admit that he was *different*. But he didn't understand them any better than they understood him.

"Why would anyone want to fight?" he'd often asked Mama Llama. "Why would you try to hurt someone else?"

Mama Llama gently nuzzled Lewie's neck. "That's just how it is," she told him. "That's how we've always worked out who's the strongest, who should be in charge. It's called *survival of the fittest,* Lewie," she explained.

But Lewie still didn't get it. He point-blank refused to fight. Whenever he was challenged Lewie just walked away. It drove his brothers crazy.

"You are a coward and a disgrace," Leo frequently told Lewie.

But Lewie didn't care. He just wasn't as competitive as his brothers. When they were younger and had played games, like dominoes or chess, Leo and Lamar always *had* to win. If they didn't, they threw their pieces on the ground and trampled them, or tried to eat the board!

"It's only a game," he told his brothers.

"The trouble with you, Lewie," they told him, "is that everything's a game *to you*."

What was wrong with that? Lewie wondered. Laughing, playing, having fun… Who wouldn't choose those things over fighting?

It wasn't that he didn't *care* about anything, or want to be good at it. There were some things he was far better at than all the others put together. One was acting; another was making people laugh. Lewie would do almost anything to make people laugh. No matter how silly it made him look, he didn't care. And that drove Lamar crazy too.

"You're an insult to the whole Llama family," he told Lewie, "an absolute embarrassment."

Latisha agreed. After Lewie's impressions of her, she was hopping mad. She contradicted herself, almost in the same breath, by telling him that he was an absolute joke and not in the least bit funny!

"No one takes you seriously," she added.

"Who cares?" shrugged Lewie. He thought his brothers and Latisha took themselves *far* too seriously.

Lewie was now standing with his twin sister, Liberty, while the three others threw insults at him.

"You're almost as bad as *her*," Latisha told Lewie.

"You're a disgrace," Leo agreed. *"Both of you."*

Lewie and Liberty didn't try to argue back. They just rolled their eyes at each other and waited for the insults to end.

"At least we know the farmer won't be choosing either of those two tomorrow," Lamar said.

"Don't make me yelp." Leo honked with pretend laughter. "They couldn't guard a pile of potatoes."

"The Clown and the Disappearing Queen? I don't think so," agreed Latisha. "I just hope next time Her Majesty gets out they don't bother bringing her back," she added nastily.

"Come on, let's go," said Lewie. "We don't have to listen to this rubbish."

Lewie and Liberty ambled off together, trying to look as if it was all water off a llama's back to them. But sometimes the insults did hit the mark and were harder to shrug off. Today felt like one of those days to Lewie.

Apart from Mama Llama, Liberty was the only member of his family that Lewie felt close to. Even though they were twins, and looked a lot like each other, they weren't at all alike in other ways. Except that they were both odd ones out.

While nobody understood Lewie's passion for acting, it was considered a pretty harmless pastime. Liberty's wasn't. Her passion got her into a lot more trouble, because Liberty liked to think of herself as an *escape artist.*

The smallest gap in the fence, the split second the gate was left unfastened, even the least likely opportunity, Liberty would turn into yet one more dash for freedom. She just couldn't help herself. Her whole family despaired of her, not to mention the farmer.

Farmer Palmer had tried to increase the security round the field. As well as that, the llama family kept a constant watch on Liberty, but she continued to plan and execute the most unexpected and daring escapes. She really seemed unstoppable.

Lewie was curious about his twin sister. "Doesn't it ever bother you," he asked, "getting into so much trouble? And all the jokes about... you know... *escaping?*"

Liberty went on chewing grass perfectly happily. She shrugged and smiled at Lewie. "Of course it does. I'd like to be like everyone else," she said. "Life would be a lot easier. But something drives me. I see a crack and I *have* to get through it. It's just who I am, I guess."

Lewie sighed heavily. It was still bothering him.

"Hey, we're all different," Liberty reminded him. "You're a llama that makes everyone smile, and that's not a small thing. You bring joy to others. It's a gift, Lewie. You should be proud of it."

At last Lewie felt cheered up by his sister's words. Deep down he knew it was true. He started to sing and did a few more backflips. It wasn't long before he was soon the centre of an admiring crowd again.

Mama and Papa Llama were watching. "You've got to love him," Mama Llama told Papa Llama. "Everyone else does."

There was no question that his father *did* love Lewie, but that didn't stop him worrying about his son. "Everyone may love him, my dear, but does anyone take him seriously?"

"Of course not," smiled Mama Llama, watching Lewie juggling with a pile of turnips. "Why would anyone want to? I mean, look at him."

"But what if he were to get chosen tomorrow?" Papa Llama asked, genuinely anxious. "Lewie couldn't look after himself, never mind a whole flock of sheep. Not to mention all those new lambs due any day now," he added.

Hmmm, the lambs were a consideration, but Mama Llama suggested that maybe it was exactly what Lewie needed, to make him grow up.

Papa Llama shook his head. "And have you forgotten *who* he'd be taking over from?" he asked gravely.

The farmer's previous Guard Llama, Livingstone, had been Papa Llama's great uncle. He had recently retired to a refuge that sounded like llama heaven and it was well deserved.

Livingstone had been an almost mythological figure who'd seen off more coyotes than any other llama in history. A bigger, braver, bolder, *scarier* llama neither of them could imagine. He was so fierce and battle-scarred that on the farm he'd been given the nickname of *The Terminator*.

"Those are awfully big footsteps for any llama to fill," said Papa Llama, "and I'm afraid to say, of all our children, Lewie would be the least likely to fill them."

Mama Llama nuzzled Papa Llama and whispered, "Look at him." Lewie was now performing a new dance that looked like a llama version of the cancan. "Do you *really* think our Lewie is going to be chosen tomorrow? Seriously? Don't worry yourself, my dear."

But Papa Llama still wasn't completely reassured. He was getting old and, in his long experience, life was full of strange and inexplicable happenings. He just prayed that this wouldn't turn out to be one of them.

Chapter Three

Surprise, Surprise

Next morning, Farmer Palmer came through the field gate even earlier than usual. Latisha and some of the other teenage llamas, never early risers, were still only half awake. But finding his new Guard Llama was an important job and the farmer was anxious to make a start. As he crossed the field he greeted the llamas by name.

"Hoi, there, Leo. Looking good, Lamar! Mornin', Mama Llama. How's Papa doing this morning?" One by one he had a word for them all. "Now then, Latisha, looks like someone got out of bed on the wrong side."

"Tchhh!" she tutted as soon as he walked on.

The farmer always made a point of teasing Latisha, which she secretly loved, but liked to pretend she didn't.

"Oh, my! Glad to see you're still here, Liberty. You look happy, as usual, Lewie."

As he toured the field of llamas, Farmer Palmer was followed by his youngest daughter, Millie, who was almost six years old. Millie was followed by her puppy, Pepsi, and her pet duck, Delilah.

After Farmer Palmer had checked out all his llamas, he gave them new feed and water. Then he turned his attention to the job at hand.

The farmer couldn't help noticing an excited buzz around the field. It amused him to think that the animals could tell something important was about to happen. Had he said that to Millie, she would have taken it entirely seriously. She was young enough to understand that animals were every bit as intelligent as humans. Obviously, they would know exactly what was going on.

"OK, let's get started," said the farmer, more to himself than anyone else. "We'll

have the front runners over here, shall we?"
And he led Leo forward first, then Lamar,
then Latisha, lining them up together,
facing the field gate.

He led me out first, thought Leo, certain
he was going to win.

Like a beauty contest, thought Lamar,
quite certain he was going to win.

'Tchhh,' tutted Latisha, wondering why
the farmer was going to all this bother
when it was perfectly clear to her that *she*
was going to win.

Millie had made a beeline for Lewie, as
usual. He was her favourite llama because
she said he always made her laugh.
Watching Lewie doing his latest tricks,

Farmer Palmer had to agree with her. Even more than the other llamas, Lewie was a real character.

Millie's pet duck, Delilah, had flown up on to Lewie's back and, as soon as the duck was securely seated, the llama trotted gently in a circle. They looked exactly as if they were practising to join the circus.

"Whoever would have believed it?" muttered the farmer.

Millie ran after them as if she too wanted a ride. So Lewie stopped and lowered his head, allowing the duck to walk along his neck. Once the bird was safely perched on his head, Lewie sank down on to his back legs to let Millie climb up in the duck's place.

Farmer Palmer looked a little nervous, but soon realised that his precious daughter was quite safe. This time Lewie trotted *even more* gently. The puppy ran between Lewie's feet, barking and complaining that he was being left out of the fun. So once again Lewie dropped his back legs to let Millie pick up the puppy too. Then they all did a triumphant lap, while the other llamas looked on, amazed.

"Isn't he wonderful, Papa!" Millie called to her father.

Mama Llama gave Papa Llama a little knowing look that said, *You see, I told you, everyone loves Lewie.*

"He's certainly a rare llama," the farmer replied. He knew Lewie to be a gentle, reliable animal, but still he was happier once he had lifted his daughter and her pets safely to the ground. Mama and Papa Llama were a little relieved too.

The farmer explained to Millie that now he had to choose one of the three llamas he'd singled out for a very important job.

"It'll take a lot to fill Livingstone's place," he told her. "This llama's going to need lots of qualities. Now, where did I put my list?"

As the farmer searched his pockets, the three shortlisted llamas prepared to show him that they each had all the necessary qualities – and more!

"Number one: physical size," the farmer read out. "He's got to be a real *big, strong* llama."

This is it, thought Leo. *This is my moment!*

The three llamas all stretched their necks, trying to appear as tall as possible. Leo and Lamar lifted themselves so high on to the tips of their toes that they both lost their balance. They collapsed sideways into Latisha so that all three llamas fell like a row of dominoes before they finally got their balance back, and their legs under control.

Millie thought it was the funniest thing she'd ever seen and laughed very loudly. The three llamas looked down their noses at the little girl and huffed. They knew she wasn't the person they needed to impress.

"Number two," Farmer Palmer read out. "A Guard Llama needs to be fit and athletic."

Leo and Lamar immediately tried to out jump one another. But then Lamar got a little overexcited. He did a few high kicks, suddenly knocking the legs from underneath his brother and sister. All three llamas again scrambled to recover themselves.

"Number three," the farmer read on. "He

needs to be *responsible, reliable* and *brave*. He'll be living away from the herd, on his own, and responsible for all those sheep and lambs..." The farmer trailed off.

Latisha was already getting fed up with this contest. Why did the farmer keep assuming the Guard Llama would be a "he"? She shook her head and tutted very loudly. "Tchhh."

Farmer Palmer was relieved to see that she at least looked like her usual self – a grumpy, bored teenager. Leo and Lamar were looking very weird. They were attempting to appear *responsible, reliable* and *brave* all at the same time. As a result, they both looked like they were about to have a funny turn.

"And number four…" concluded the farmer. "Probably the most important of all – *intelligence*."

Now that's more like it, thought Latisha. *Here's my chance.*

Her brothers, in addition to the other expressions they were already trying to show on their faces, now added *intelligence*.

Oh, boy, thought Lewie. Those two could definitely have used some acting lessons from him. For once, Latisha agreed. She thought her brothers each looked like they were about to lay an egg! Farmer Palmer folded up his list, still looking undecided.

"But, Papa," Millie told him. "It's

obvious. There's only one llama with all those qualities. That's Lewie."

It was as if someone had struck a loud gong. There was a moment's absolute silence... Then the name of Lewie seemed to echo around the field: *Lewie, Lewie, Lewie, Lewie, Lewie...*

Mama and Papa Llama gasped and leant on one another for support. The three shortlisted llamas froze, then stood to attention. Their ears, like question marks, rose up as if waiting for the farmer's answer.

The answer seemed to be slow in coming. The farmer looked flummoxed. It hadn't even occurred to him to consider the younger llama. He did now, but only for a second. Then he shook his head and laughed. "Oh, no, I don't think so. Not Lewie, darlin'."

Lewie's parents relaxed. Leo, Lamar and Latisha relaxed. Most of all, Lewie relaxed.

"But why not, Papa?" Millie persisted. "He's the best; he's so funny!"

"Funny won't keep the coyotes away," replied her father.

"He's *big* and *strong* enough," she argued. This was true. Lewie wasn't much shorter than his brothers, and was as tall as Latisha.

"And look at all the clever tricks he can do," Millie continued. The farmer had to admit this was true too.

"And he's *reliable* and *responsible*."

All the other llamas nodded in agreement. They'd gradually gathered from all corners of the field as they realised that something quite unexpected might be about to happen.

Millie had her own reasons for taking Lewie's side. Like him, she had older brothers and sisters who were always bossing her about. Like him, she was often told she couldn't do things. She'd seen him elbowed out by these three before now.

"And he's very *intelligent*. Anyone can see that," she added.

As Lewie heard Millie listing all his qualities he began to feel quite proud. It was unusual for him to hear anything really positive said about him. Oh, yes, people loved to laugh at him, but no one had ever told him he was *intelligent* before. Lewie found himself standing a little taller, a little prouder, looking a little more serious.

The farmer noticed this and wondered how it was he hadn't spotted it before.

But then he looked back at the other three llamas. They still looked far more suitable. He was sorry to disappoint his daughter, but...

"Maybe next time, when Lewie's grown a bit more," he told Millie.

Now that they were back in the frame, Leo, Lamar and Latisha started jostling for the farmer's attention again.

Leo, as the biggest, hustled his way to the front. Or he would have done had Lamar not stretched out his foot and tripped him up. Lamar took the opportunity to take centre stage himself. He pushed Latisha roughly aside with his bigger bottom. He took up what he hoped was a dignified pose, right under the farmer's nose.

By now Latisha had put up with just about enough of her brother's nonsense. She quietly dropped her head and closed her teeth on Lamar's bottom – and bit him *hard*. Lamar let out a very undignified honking sound, right into the farmer's face. Farmer Palmer was not impressed.

He was even less impressed when the three llamas started ramming, spitting and neck-wrestling each other, as if their lives depended on it.

Farmer Palmer shook his head, clearly disappointed in them. The one thing he didn't need was an aggressive, unruly, unreliable llama as his guard.

"OK, then. Let's give him a try. It looks

like Lewie's our new Guard Llama," the farmer announced.

A sudden hush came over the whole herd. The three fighting llamas stopped, then drooped as their big chance passed them by. And Lewie, who hadn't expected to get the job and didn't even know if he wanted it, got picked out from the whole herd.

There wasn't a moment to say his goodbyes. Lewie was led away by the farmer and his utterly delighted daughter, followed by her puppy and her duck.

The whole Llama family was left in a state of absolute shock. Mama and Papa Llama couldn't believe it. All Papa

Llama knew was that one of those strange and inexplicable happenings he'd been dreading had just taken place.

Chapter Four

Lewie No-Mates

Not too far away, in a burrow in the woods, two coyotes were trying to sleep. At least, one of them was. Captain Coyote blinked his eyes and realised it was still daylight, darn it, and that young nephew of his was wide awake.

Cupcake was far too excited to sleep. "Tell me again, sir," he begged, "about what it tastes like."

Captain Coyote huffed and puffed and gave up trying to sleep. For what felt like the hundredth time, he described to his nephew that first taste of new young spring lamb. How *tender* it was, how it *melted* in the mouth. How different it was to tough old mutton. How there was nothing in the world like it, especially smothered in—

"Mint sauce!" chorused Cupcake.

"Exactly so," Captain snapped. "Now, can a person get some sleep around here?"

"And we'll really get some tonight?" Cupcake asked excitedly.

"Or tomorrow," Captain promised, "but very soon. *If* we can get some sleep."

Cupcake, finally satisfied, quietened down.

To tell the truth, Captain hadn't done much hunting himself in a long while. He was an old coyote now. He'd only come out of retirement as a favour, to teach this young nephew a few tricks of the trade.

Until recently Captain would never have considered hunting around here, on Farmer Palmer's land. Not with such a young, inexperienced pup as Cupcake alongside. But he'd heard news that the old Guard Llama was gone. Been *retired* was the rumour he'd heard. So it would be plain sailing – a quick in and out with a couple of young lambs between their teeth. Couldn't be simpler. Captain had to admit to feeling a little excited himself.

He looked fondly over at his nephew, already asleep and dreaming. Captain wondered briefly what kind of animal the new Guard Llama might be. But then, whoever it was wouldn't be a patch on his old enemy, *The Terminator*. Apart from Livingstone, there wasn't a llama on four legs that could stop Captain Coyote. No, siree.

☆

Coyotes were the last thing on Lewie's mind at that moment. He was having enough trouble just managing sheep. He'd had no idea how difficult they could be. He'd thought sheep were quiet, shy creatures, not very bright, but simple and easy to manage. How wrong he had been. He'd spent the whole morning trying to get to know one or two of them – without any success.

"Hi, there, everyone, I'm *Lewie*," he'd said nervously, but in a friendly way. Lewie liked to think he was good at making friends, a bit of a llama charmer, in fact. But the sheep had completely blanked him. It wasn't a good feeling being faced with a sea of blinking eyes, staring dumbly back at him.

Blink... blink... blink... times fifty! Not a single smile between them. They were the worst audience Lewie had ever had.

He gave it another go, trying to appear more confident than he was actually feeling. "Really pleased to meet you all!

I'm your new friendly llama, all singing, all dancing... Boy, are we going to have some fun together!"

Blink... blink... blink...

Without a sound, the sheep turned their backs and wandered off in small groups. All heavily pregnant, they moved very slowly, but with one aim – to get as far away from Lewie as they could.

The young llama was already feeling lonely, separated from his family for the first time. He stood there now, holding back a tear or two. But rather than feel sorry for himself, Lewie tried to imagine what his older brothers, or Latisha, would do. They wouldn't just go and cry in a corner.

"Come on, now," he told himself. "You can't give up that easily."

Lewie moved briskly to the nearest group of sheep. He decided to use a more forceful approach.

"OK, let's try this again," he barked in a much louder voice. "My name's Lewie! L-E-W-I-E!"

It came out even louder than he'd intended and echoed around the field, startling the sheep into a stampede. They raced away, bleating, as fast as their heavy bellies would allow.

Lewie sighed, but he still wasn't ready to give up. He moved on to another group of six sheep standing nearby, idly nibbling the grass. Maybe the loud voice had been a mistake. He wouldn't repeat that.

"Look here," he said, trying to sound kindly, "you're probably feeling shy. I'm feeling shy too."

This was greeted with yet more blinking, but no other response.

Lewie wondered if maybe they didn't understand him. Maybe they didn't speak *Llama*. He decided to use his acting skills. Pointing dramatically to himself with his foreleg, he spoke very slowly as if he were trying to communicate with someone from another planet.

"My… name… is… Lewie!" he said. "What's… your… name?"

Blink… blink… blink… times six.

Lewie was about ready to stop trying when one of the sheep suddenly said, "I'm Shirley. This is Sheila… Shelley… Shula… Shona…" Each sheep blinked as her name was spoken. "And this –" she indicated the last one, a much bigger sheep than the others – "is Ginger."

"Ginger?" asked Lewie, surprised. The sheep was, in fact, not ginger at all but a muddy brown colour.

"Not all sheep have to behave like sheep, you know," said Ginger in a much bossier voice than the others.

"…sheep, you know," repeated Sheila.

"…you know," echoed Shula.

Lewie didn't know what to make of the sheep, but he smiled and tried to look friendly.

"So?" Ginger asked him. "What's your story?"

"…your story?" asked Shelley.

"…story?" echoed Shona.

"I'm your new Guard Llama," Lewie said, pleased to be having a conversation at last. The sheep looked blank again and started to blink.

"I'm here to protect you all… from coyotes… and things…?" Lewie trailed off. The sheep's faces first registered suspicion, then disbelief.

Ginger started to laugh, then all the other sheep joined in. They were laughing so much their heavy bellies shook from side to side.

"Oh, stop, stop," Ginger begged. "This minute!"

"...this minute!" the other sheep echoed.

Lewie didn't say a word. He waited for the sheep to stop laughing. When they finally realised that he *wasn't* joking, they did stop. Then they turned on him.

"*You*... are going to guard *us?*" asked Ginger.

"...guard us?" echoed Shona.

"You – all on your own?" Ginger asked again, waving a foreleg at him.

"…your own?" echoed Shirley.

"You mean to say that Livingstone – a legend in his own lifetime – has retired and in his place we've got *you*?" Ginger said.

"…*you*?" echoed Sheila.

None of the sheep were laughing now. They were looking *terrified*! And Lewie could see their point. They were about to have lambs. In fact, as he looked around the field, he could see one or two sheep lying on the ground already. Of course they were nervous, if not for themselves, for their newborn lambs. Lewie wished he could reassure them – tell them he was more than a match for any crafty coyotes out there. Maybe, if he'd had a chance to talk to *The Terminator*, the old llama could have given him some advice.

"What was he like, Livingstone?" Lewie asked lamely. "Did you all like him?"

"Of course we didn't *like* him," Ginger snapped. "He was one *scary* llama."

"...*scary*," echoed Shelley.

"The lambs used to shake whenever he came near," said Ginger.

"...*shake*," echoed Shula.

"Mine used to wet the bed," Shirley admitted.

"We didn't need

to *like* him," Ginger insisted. "But we trusted him. He was a *Guard Llama!*"

"...*Guard Llama*," the other sheep echoed.

"Now there's *no one* to protect us," Ginger bleated.

"...*no one* to protect us," the others repeated.

Their words were soon picked up by other sheep and travelled around the field like wildfire through a forest. Panic spread throughout the whole flock and no one felt more gripped by it than Lewie!

As the day wore on, Lewie felt as lonely, rejected and inadequate as he'd ever felt. He looked longingly over to the llama field and wished with all his heart that he were still there. He knew it was probably the biggest sign of failure, but he couldn't help himself. Lewie called over to his family for help.

"They won't even talk to me. What should I do?" he begged.

Mama and Papa Llama had been keeping a close eye on Lewie. They knew he wasn't getting on too well. Now it was time for some sound advice.

Mama Llama tried first to be encouraging, to build up Lewie's confidence.

"You can do it, Lewie," she said. "Give it time. Be yourself. They'll soon come to love you..." Then she added, not quite so confidently, "...and respect you."

"Never mind all that," Papa Llama huffed. "You've got to be strong, my boy," he called to Lewie. "Take charge. Show 'em who's boss! Earn their respect."

"Yeah, bang a few heads together!" Leo shouted in agreement.

"Kick 'em into shape!" shouted Lamar.

"Tchhh!" said Latisha. "They're just dumb sheep. Tell them anything and they'll believe it."

After all this conflicting advice, Lewie felt more confused than ever.

As his family wandered away from the fence, only Liberty was left.

"Hang in there, Lew," she called. "You

know you can do it. Stick to what you're good at, and believe in yourself."

This at last helped Lewie to feel a bit more positive.

As he looked around, even more of the sheep were starting to lie down to deliver their lambs, so he decided to leave them in peace for now. But tomorrow he was determined to do better.

As darkness fell and the sheep and their new lambs settled down to sleep, Lewie tried hard to stay awake. He was supposed to be on guard, after all. But it had been a long and tiring day and he soon felt sleep closing in on him.

Just as he was drifting off, he was startled

awake by a chorus of high-pitched yelps, cries and howls. It sounded as if a pack of wild animals was approaching. Lewie shot to his feet, immediately alert, his heart racing…

But the cries and howls were quickly followed by a burst of laughter coming from the llama field.

"Got you there, Lewie," his brothers and Latisha called out. "Goodnight. Sleep tight. Don't let the coyotes bite…"

Back in the woods, Captain Coyote had just finished his first lesson on *Tactics for Outwitting the Average Guard Llama*. It had been a rather long lesson and he'd had to nudge his nephew awake several times during it. But now at last he felt they were ready to put some of this learning into action.

The two coyotes crept silently out of their burrow. Well, almost silently. Cupcake was far too excited for silence.

"Now, hush," Captain warned him. "First rule of hunting: *not a whisper!*"

Immediately, they were greeted by the full-throated call of what sounded like a whole pack of prairie dogs, or possibly other coyotes.

Captain Coyote stopped dead in his tracks. It seemed like they might have competition. Well, there was no shame in being cautious, especially with a new young pup by his side.

"Back to base, young laddo," said Captain Coyote. "Sounds like someone got there before us. Always remember, my boy, *He who retreats lives to hunt another day.*"

Chapter Five

How to Win Friends, or Not

When Lewie woke the next morning he found the field littered with newly born lambs. Just the sight of them would have lifted his mood, but Lewie was already feeling much more positive.

After his family's silly joke the night

before, Lewie had taken a long time to get to sleep. Lying awake, he'd thought about what his twin sister, Liberty, had said – about sticking to what he was good at. Now he knew what he needed to do to win the sheep over. He needed to entertain them. He'd already worked out a little programme. He was really looking forward to it.

Lewie did a quick tour of the field. First he admired the new lambs, then he told all the mother sheep that there was going to be a show. They should come over to the middle of the field in half an hour.

"And bring the new lambs," he told them.

As the sheep began to drift over, Lewie cried, "Roll up! Roll up, for the Greatest One-Llama Show in the World: Tricks, Jokes, Singing, Dancing and Death-defying Stunts…" he promised them.

OK, that last bit might be an exaggeration, but Lewie was determined to impress those *blinking* sheep – if it was the last thing he did!

Meanwhile, in his burrow, Captain Coyote was wide awake and this time he couldn't blame his nephew. Cupcake was sucking his paw and dreaming of tender, juicy spring lamb. The old coyote had promised his nephew he would taste it and he was not about to break that promise. They'd been disappointed last night, but next time he wanted to be sure nothing would go wrong.

So Captain decided to do a little exploring on his own, to check out this new Guard Llama. While Cupcake was safely asleep, Captain slipped out without a sound. Startled for a moment by the brightness of the unfamiliar daylight, he headed into the shade and carefully skirted the farm.

Lewie was glad to see that quite a few sheep had taken up his invitation. They were standing nearby, nibbling the grass as if they had just happened to be there. They weren't really interested, but Lewie didn't let this discourage him. He would soon win them over.

He started with a couple of song-and-dance numbers. Lewie put his heart and soul into them, as he always did. But even the brilliance of his tap-dancing was greeted with the sheep's usual blank, then blinking stares.

Well, singing and dancing wasn't everyone's cup of tea, so Lewie decided that a few jokes might go down better. He began with one or two that always amused the llamas.

"What do you get if you cross a sheep with a kangaroo?" Lewie asked.

Blink… blink… blink…

"A woolly jumper!"

Blink… blink… blink…

"OK, what do you get if you cross a sheep with *a frog?*" Lewie asked. "A *green* woolly jumper."

He beamed at the sheep. The sheep blinked back.

Lewie thought that perhaps they didn't understand when the joke was finished. So next time he decided he would add, *boom-boom*.

"Where do sheep go for their holidays?" he asked. "The Baa-haa-maas! *Boom-boom!*"

But the sheep still only blinked.

Lewie tried one last joke. A *knock-knock* this time.

"Knock, knock!" he said.

"Who's there?" Lewie answered himself. "Sheep go. Sheep go who? No – sheep go baaa!" he said, even making himself smile. Surely the sheep must get that joke.

But they didn't.

Blink... blink... blink...

Lewie was seriously beginning to think that sheep had *no sense of humour*! Was there *nothing* that could make these stony-faced animals crack a smile? But he felt sure that even *they* couldn't resist his speciality. It was time to bring out his biggest weapon – *Lewie's Mimes*.

Lewie started with *Llama tripping over a banana skin,*

then Llama doing the splits,

Llama sitting on a

whoopee cushion,

Llama standing on

his own foot

and falling down a hole,

and finished with *Llama*
gets a custard pie in the face.

Still not even a single smile.

Blink… blink… blink…

In desperation Lewie went straight into *Llama does a lingering death scene.*

For the first time the sheep began to show real interest. When Lewie fell to the floor for the second time – and didn't get up – they all moved in towards him. Keeping their lambs behind them, the sheep pressed forward for a closer look. Finally, Lewie had their attention!

But when he leapt up and cried, "Ta-daa!" the sheep scuttled back nervously. Then they wandered off, muttering and grumbling to themselves, as if he'd cheated them in some way. The sheep looked hugely disappointed.

But the most disappointed animal by far was Lewie.

Captain Coyote, who'd seen the whole performance, didn't feel disappointed – he felt surprised, confused, *bewildered*. He'd met many llamas in his time, but he'd never seen one like this. His first thought was that Lewie was completely crazy.

On the other hand, Captain Coyote was old enough and wise enough to realise that you should *never underestimate your enemy*. Farmers were crafty and they often had very cunning tricks up their sleeves. But if Lewie was the best trick Farmer Palmer could come up with, then those lambs were just asking to be eaten. He might as well hang signs round their necks saying: **FREE FOOD. COME AND GET ME!**

Captain made his way back to the burrow in high spirits. Tonight, he and Cupcake would feast on tender, young, spring lamb, or his name wasn't Captain Cornelius Columbus Coyote. No, siree!

Lewie knew that he really shouldn't go to his family for help yet again. But he desperately needed a kind word from another animal. He hung longingly over the fence, trying to attract their attention. But Mama and Papa Llama had given strict instructions that no one was to talk to Lewie for the next few days.

"That boy has to learn to stand on his own four feet," Papa Llama explained. "It'll only make it harder if he keeps coming back to us. Trust me, this is for his own good."

"Sometimes you have to be cruel to be kind," Mama Llama agreed, although she didn't sound entirely convinced. She found it hard when they heard Lewie calling, but even she turned away and headed to the furthest side of the llama field.

Lewie felt completely abandoned. But much later, when she was sure no one was looking, Liberty answered Lewie's calls. She tried to be helpful, suggesting different things he might do to win the sheep over. But each time, Lewie said, "Tried it," or "Done that," or "They didn't get that either."

Before she could say any more words of encouragement Liberty spotted Papa Llama heading in her direction.

"Gotta go, Lew," she called hastily. "Hang in there. I'll try to get out and come and see you."

Lewie didn't want his sister getting into more trouble. "Better not," he called back, but Liberty had already trotted away. Lewie was alone again.

But despite how sad he was feeling, Lewie couldn't ignore all the new life around him.

He was amazed at how quickly the lambs were up on their little legs and running about. He was surprised too at how quickly the mother sheep seemed to forget about them. Ginger and her friends were all back in their group. They were nibbling the grass and gossiping – *probably about him* – leaving the lambs to their own devices.

Once or twice it was lucky that Lewie was there to lead them away from danger. He nudged the little runaways back to their mothers. Not that the mother sheep bothered to thank Lewie. They were all still giving him the cold shoulder. But the new lambs quite quickly realised how interesting Lewie was – and how much fun.

They followed him wherever he went. Soon he'd collected quite a fan club.

Whenever Lewie did anything they liked, the lambs giggled and ran after him bleating, "Again! Again! Again!"

Lewie found that all his jokes and tricks were new and funny to the lambs. Whereas the sheep had been the hardest audience he'd ever had, the lambs were the easiest. He began to feel that at last he was making some friends.

Encouraged by his success, Lewie decided to work out some new tricks and different musical numbers to amuse the lambs the next day.

As soon as the flock settled down to sleep,

Lewie found a quiet corner where he could rehearse. He was starting to feel more like his old self: light and funny and confident.

Lewie pretended there was a large, silent, *hidden* audience he was determined to impress. The moon shone between the trees, creating a huge spotlight – as if it had been ordered specially for him. Lewie stepped into it and started with a big, show-stopping song-and-dance number. At the end of it he took a bow before making his exit, imagining the cheering and clapping from his invisible audience.

After a short pause to get his breath, Lewie stepped into the moonlight again where it came through the trees at a

different angle. This time he practised some new impressions. Lewie imagined himself as an entirely different llama – bigger, braver, much scarier… He was a little too good at that. The sheep might think *The Terminator* was back. In fact, he made a mental note to tone it down for tomorrow. He didn't want the lambs too scared to sleep at night.

For the next hour Lewie slipped in and out of the moonlight, creating a whole cast of characters – all very real and all completely different. Or so it would have seemed to an audience – if he'd had one!

What Lewie didn't realise was – he actually had.

Chapter Six

Breakthrough at Last

The coyotes had left the burrow as soon as it was dark to make their way to the farm. Cupcake, excited at the thought of his first taste of lamb, couldn't stop chattering.

"How many lambs can you eat, sir?" he asked Captain. "I could eat one hundred all by myself. No... two hundred. Three hundred!"

"Quiet, young fella," Captain warned him. "Let's not give ourselves away. Remember what I told you about *the element of surprise!*"

Captain hardly cared how many he ate tonight; if things went well they'd be eating lamb *every* night from now on. Growing fat and lazy. Why not, with only that feeble young llama to stop them?

Suddenly, both coyotes stopped dead. Lit by a beam of moonlight, they could see the new Guard Llama leaping about, throwing himself into the air. Captain put a paw on Cupcake's shoulder and drew the young pup into the shadows.

Then they watched Lewie, trying to make sense of the llama's strange, incomprehensible behaviour. Was this some new tactic to frighten them off? Captain wondered. Well, it wasn't going to work. While the llama was busy with his fooling about, they'd cunningly double back and find a new point of entry. They'd be in and out and he wouldn't even notice.

So imagine Captain's surprise when, on their second attempt, they came upon *another* llama in another beam of moonlight. This one *seemed* twice as big – and twice as fierce. Cupcake thought it looked like a *monster-llama*. The little pup hid behind the old coyote, shaking. Captain felt rather nervous himself.

Once again they retreated, skirting a little further round. But at each new attempt, they met *another*, *different* llama! Or so it looked to Captain.

Hmmm. He'd clearly underestimated the farmer. But now it all began to make sense. How could Farmer Palmer replace his old Guard Llama with just one animal? No, siree. They didn't make them like *The Terminator* any more.

"They've swapped him for a whole army of llamas! Darn it!" Captain told Cupcake. This called for a new plan of action. "Sorry, young fella," he told his disappointed nephew. "We'll have to leave it till tomorrow. But don't you worry. Captain promised you new, young, spring lamb and new, young, spring lamb is what you're gonna get. Depend on it. We'll be back!"

After his late evening rehearsing, Lewie was a little slow waking up the next morning. He'd have liked a bit of a lie-in, actually, but he didn't get the chance. Before his eyes were even open, Lewie was surrounded by young lambs tugging at him.

"Lewie, wake up! Lewie! Lewie! Lewie!" they squealed.

They climbed on to his back, hanging from his shaggy coat. There were so many he couldn't count them.

Lewie was still trying to learn all their names. He knew that Shirley had called her lamb Shane, Sheila's was Shep, Shelley's was Sheba, Shona's was Shah, Shula's was…

No, he couldn't remember.

"Shoo," bleated the smallest one. "I'm Shoo!" It sounded like a little sneeze.

Lewie wasn't surprised to learn that Ginger's lamb was called… Bertie.

It was Bertie who was now bouncing on Lewie's back, then using his tail to slide down. The others soon started to copy him. All except Shoo, who stared intently up at Lewie and asked, "Why do you look so different?"

"Because I'm not a sheep," Lewie explained. "I'm a llama. Like all those over there." He pointed towards the llama field.

"Why aren't you in that field with the others?" Shep asked.

"Because I'm here to protect you all," he told them. "I'm your Guard Llama." Lewie was surprised how proud that made him feel.

"Who're you protecting us from?" asked Shoo.

"Oh… wild dogs… wolves… coyotes…" Lewie said vaguely, trying to make it sound light and unimportant.

"But why?" Shoo asked.

Lewie hesitated. "In case they try to eat you," he said quietly.

"*Eat us!*" the lambs all shrieked. "Why would they eat *us*?"

Lewie looked at the scared little faces and shook his head sadly. "I can't imagine," he said honestly. And he really couldn't. Lewie was a vegetarian, like them. His eyes filled with tears at the thought of anything eating his new little friends.

"So how will you protect us?" asked Bertie.

Lewie felt ashamed that he didn't have a plan. He felt more ashamed that he didn't even have the words to reassure the lambs. Instead, he decided to distract them by changing the subject.

"Who wants to learn some tricks?" Lewie asked, and suddenly all thoughts of coyotes disappeared.

Half a dozen lambs bounced up and down on the spot, bleating, "Me! Me! Me! Me! Me! Me!"

Lewie lined up the lambs facing him and showed them some simple moves. The lambs tried to copy him, but they were far too excited. They kept tripping over their own feet, or each other's. They landed in a giggling, woolly heap.

"Whoops! I fell over!" squealed Shoo.

"You fell over me!" squealed Shep.

"No, *you* fell over *me*," Bertie insisted.

"Let's try again," said Lewie patiently. "We'll take it a bit more slowly this time."

The lambs had lots of energy and were very keen to please Lewie. They soon picked up simple moves, so he decided to try something a little more ambitious. He taught the lambs to do forward rolls, then backflips, even some balancing tricks. They were so good at these that Lewie finally showed them how to make a Lamb

Pyramid. He was very pleased with them.

The only problem was Bertie, who insisted on being the one on top. Unfortunately, Bertie was the biggest of the lambs and clearly needed to be on the bottom row.

"Look here, Bertie," Lewie told him quietly, "the others are nothing like as strong as you. They need you to hold them up. It's the key job, you know, being the anchor lamb."

Bertie's little chest puffed up with pride as he took his place in the middle.

"I'm the anchor lamb," he kept telling everyone. "It's the key job, you know."

Of course, all this had to stop whenever Farmer Palmer showed up. Then Lewie strutted around the field trying to look strong and serious and *in charge*. He thought it was best if the farmer didn't know everything that happened on his farm, especially in this field.

But Lewie had no such worries about Millie. He knew the little girl understood animals even better than her father did. She wouldn't think it was odd to see them dancing or singing or doing tricks. In fact, Millie had taken to spending most of her time with them now in the sheep pasture. She didn't interfere or try to join in. She just liked to watch Lewie playing with the lambs.

When her father came to collect her for lunch, Millie told him, "See, Papa, didn't I tell you Lewie was a llama in a million?"

Farmer Palmer was reserving judgement. "Maybe," he said. "But this llama still has to prove himself. Wait till there's a coyote attack, then we'll see."

But despite the farmer's reservations about Lewie, he was finally making a better impression with the sheep. They were more than happy to have Lewie looking after their lambs while they put their hooves up.

"He's very good with them," sighed Shirley contentedly.

"…good with them," echoed Sheila, Shelley, Shona and Shula.

"I said, right from the start, he was going to be *wonderful*," Ginger insisted. "If you all remember."

"…remember," echoed the others, although, to tell the truth, they didn't.

Lewie decided the lambs were good

enough to put on a little show for everyone. At the end of the day, when the flock gathered round, Lewie cried, "Ladies and Gentle-lambs, allow me to introduce – for your delight and entertainment – Sheba, Shep, Shane, Shah, Shoo and… Bertie!"

The six little lambs came on doing somersaults, forward rolls, backflips, cartwheels, even the splits, and finally their party piece – the Lamb Pyramid.

Lewie didn't expect the stunned silence that followed. *Oh, not again*, he thought. But then came a trickle of applause that turned into a tidal wave of bleating and stamping of hooves. Finally, the whole flock was showing its complete appreciation.

Lewie was delighted. The mother sheep patted their lambs and tried to take full credit for their talents.

"He takes after me, you know," bleated Shirley.

"…after me," repeated Sheila.

"I was a bit of a gymnast," said Shelley,  "when I was younger."

"…younger," Shona agreed.

More and more lambs crowded round Lewie, asking if they could learn some tricks too and be in a show. In fact, none of the lambs would agree to go to bed until Lewie promised that tomorrow he would teach them all tricks, songs, dances... whatever they fancied.

Lewie was glad to see that the lambs were far too tired and excited after their performance to remember anything he'd said about coyotes. He slowly patrolled the field. As he passed, groups of sheep and their lambs sang out, "Goodnight, Lewie. See you tomorrow."

"Goodnight. Sleep tight," Lewie called back. He added under his breath, "And please don't let the coyotes bite."

The coyotes were almost close enough to

have heard him. They'd come out early to make sure they were prepared. If he was going to take on all these different llamas, Captain wanted to know exactly how many there were.

Cupcake wasn't used to being up and about in daylight. He was having a bit of trouble staying awake – until he saw the performing lambs. The young pup was so excited to see them doing their tricks that he completely forgot about wanting to eat one. Hidden in the fern and bracken, on the edge of the field, Cupcake tried to copy them. He rolled around doing somersaults, then lay giggling helplessly when he got them wrong. Captain Coyote was not amused.

"Concentrate, young fella," he growled. "No time for this tomfoolery. Hunting's a serious business."

Cupcake jumped to attention, at least for a minute or two.

Captain was puzzled again. Something odd was going on. As dusk fell and Lewie did his round of the field, Captain and Cupcake followed him at a safe distance. There could be no doubt that, tonight at least, there was only one llama – that crazy dancing llama. So where had all the others gone?

Captain wasn't one of those old-fashioned, superstitious characters who believed in magic. He was a modern coyote that moved with the times. He trusted what his eyes told him. And his eyes told him there was only one llama on guard – and not much of a llama at that. Now might well be the perfect time to attack.

But, darn it! When Captain looked round he discovered his nephew curled up in a ball, fast asleep. The young pup had completely overexcited himself and was worn out. Captain snapped his teeth in frustration. Another chance missed. But then he shrugged and lifted the sleeping bundle on to his back and headed for home. There was always tomorrow.

"Don't you worry," he whispered to Lewie, through gritted canine teeth. "Next time nothing will stop us. No, siree."

Chapter Seven

Who's the Most Popular Personality

Any doubts Lewie still had about his popularity – with the lambs at least – were put to rest the next morning. He was tugged to his feet by a whole army of them, eager to start learning to perform like their friends.

"Lewie! Lewie! Lewie! We want to act…
do tricks… be in a show…"

But to Lewie's surprise it wasn't only
the lambs that wanted his attention, it
was their mothers too. In small groups the
sheep drew Lewie aside.

"I wouldn't mind trying a few of those
tricks," Shirley bleated.

"…tricks," Sheila and Shelley repeated.

"I've always fancied dancing," Shona
admitted shyly.

"…dancing," Shula echoed.

"Dancing! I could teach you all a thing
or two about dancing," Ginger bleated.

The other sheep looked at her blankly.

"Where do you think I got this name from?" she demanded.

Blink… blink… blink…

"Don't tell me you've never heard of Ginger Rogers?" Ginger said, amazed.

The sheep stared blankly again. Obviously, *they* hadn't, but Lewie had. Ginger Rogers was one of Lewie's idols and the greatest dancer ever, apart from Fred Astaire maybe. Lewie couldn't quite imagine Ginger the sheep being as light on her hooves as Ginger Rogers, but he was happy to be proved wrong on that matter.

Soon, more and more sheep were nudging the lambs aside, demanding to be included. Lewie began to see that the little show he'd been planning was rapidly turning into a complete extravaganza. He'd never had this kind of response from the llamas. Maybe they'd enjoyed watching *him*, but they'd never been interested in performing themselves. This was the breakthrough Lewie had been waiting for. He couldn't remember ever feeling happier.

But it wasn't going to be easy. He had to become quite bossy at times to keep all those lambs and sheep in order.

"OK, OK, let's get organised," Lewie shouted over the excited bleating of the flock. "You lot over here." First, he put them into small groups and then sent them off to practise. He chose one of his more experienced performing lambs – Shane, Shep, Shah, Sheba, Shoo or Bertie – to lead each group. The lambs were determined to live up to this huge responsibility.

"We won't let you down," Bertie promised, and the others echoed.

"I know you won't," Lewie assured them. He felt so proud watching the enthusiastic lambs leading their little groups away.

The thing that surprised Lewie most was the variety of talent that these straight-faced sheep had been hiding under their big woolly coats. They were soon competing to show Lewie all the things they could do.

There were singers – everything from opera to popular songs – dancers, jugglers,

even a ventriloquist. There were sheep that
fancied themselves as clowns, or comedians.
One or two, Lewie noticed, had stolen his
jokes, but he didn't mention it. There were
acrobatic sheep and sheep that were good

at mime. There was a strongman-sheep, a yodelling sheep and a sheep who could do magic tricks. There was even a sheep who thought she might be a hypnotist.

Lewie found that Ginger hadn't been exaggerating either. She really was very nimble on her hooves. And she proved to be as good at teaching the steps to her friends. Of course, it helped that Ginger was naturally bossy.

"Follow me!" she bleated. "And smile, everyone! Don't just stand there *blinking*!"

Lewie moved from group to group, giving the sheep advice, suggesting different steps, extra tricks, better timing. Whatever Lewie said, the sheep and lambs listened and nodded. They all did exactly as they were told. They were soon like a well-drilled army with Lewie as their general.

"All in time, now: 1 – 2 – 3 – 4…" Lewie rehearsed them over and over until they were absolutely perfect.

But no matter how hard they were working, everyone was having FUN!

Lewie had never seen so many smiling sheep, while the lambs were almost bursting with excitement.

"Look at me! Look at me! Look at me!" they bleated, skipping and dancing around the field.

"Wonderful!" Lewie told them. "You're all wonderful!'

Millie was having almost as much fun just watching. She'd been hanging over the fence all morning, as usual. She didn't really know for sure quite what was going on, but she knew it was something *amazing*. She understood that she had to stay outside, as an onlooker, but she would have given almost anything to become one of the animals for the day.

Over in the llama field, the llamas were watching too. They were intrigued to see what the sheep were up to. The whole family was pressed against the fence, trying to get a closer look. One or two were even wishing they could get involved.

Mama Llama was so happy to see Lewie

having a good time and making new friends, but Papa Llama was *not* happy. Far from it.

"You have to admit, they do seem to like him now," Mama Llama pointed out.

"Like him? *Like him!* He doesn't need to be *liked*," Papa Llama exploded, "the boy needs to be *feared*. Unless he's planning to make friends with the coyotes, then tickle them to death. What's the point of all this drama nonsense? He shouldn't be fooling about, he should be *preparing*. What if the coyotes come tonight? Will he be ready?"

Lewie's older brothers and Latisha agreed with their papa.

"If it were *my* flock, those coyotes

wouldn't dare attack," said Leo, puffing himself up. "Word would have got round by now – 'Don't touch those sheep,'" he said, pretending to be a coyote, "'their Guard Llama's *scary*.'"

"*Scary?*" Lamar sneered. Was that the best word his brother could come up with? If it were *his* flock he'd have a bigger reputation than that.

"I'd be more than *scary*..." Lamar bragged, searching for a better description. He considered *ferocious, dangerous, awesome,* then he finally said, "I'd be... *dynamite!*" Lamar was so pleased with it that he said it again, spitting the word between his teeth. "*Dynamite!*"

Latisha tossed her head and rolled her eyes. "Tchhh," she tutted.

Her brothers were such idiots. If it were her flock and it came to a fight, she wouldn't be afraid. But it wouldn't come to a fight, because she'd have a plan worked out. *A strategy!*

"I'd outwit those pea-brained coyotes," she told her brothers, "because, unlike you two *dodos*, I have a brain."

"Children, children!" Mama Llama complained. She didn't like to hear this bickering. Fighting was one thing, but she really didn't approve of them being mean to one another, especially when they were being unkind to Lewie. It upset her to hear his father being so critical of him too, just when Lewie was looking so much happier! And so were the sheep.

"See how they all pay attention to him," she pointed out. "See how they listen to his every word. He's clearly in charge. Those sheep look like they'd follow him anywhere…"

"Yeah," Papa Llama sighed, "straight into a coyote's jaws."

Liberty, who'd been watching and listening, could see all sides of the argument. Like Mama Llama, she was happy to see Lewie finally settling in and making friends. But Papa was right too. He needed to be ready if coyotes attacked, and

Liberty wasn't absolutely sure he would be.

She began to hatch a back-up plan for Lewie.

In their burrow, Captain Coyote was teaching Cupcake another important lesson. This time it was history: *Lives of Great Coyotes and the Llamas they've Beaten.* Of course, he was far too modest to have included himself in that list. But Captain had a host of wonderful tales to tell of some of the Great Coyotes he'd met. So he was surprised, and a little disappointed, that Cupcake wasn't more enthralled by his stories. The truth was, his nephew was barely even listening. He seemed to be far more interested in all that nonsense he'd seen the lambs doing the day before. Cupcake was continually humming, or jigging about, doing silly moves he'd copied from the lambs. Captain realised he was only a pup and allowances had to be made, but still…

"Time to concentrate, young fella," he told Cupcake. "Tonight's a big night. We've waited too long already. There's only one thing standing between us and as much lamb as we can eat. And that thing is a feeble, harmless, idiotic young llama that's too busy dancing and playing the fool to do his job. *Lewie!* What kind of a name's that for a Guard Llama? I ask you. But tonight he'd better watch out, because he's about to meet his doom."

Captain was sounding much more confident than he was really feeling. He hadn't shared any of his own private doubts with his nephew. Doubts that had kept him awake for most of the day. These were very unsettling thoughts that he was trying hard to ignore. But the more he pushed them away, the more they kept coming back.

On the surface, Lewie appeared completely harmless, but this made Captain all the more suspicious. He still had an uneasy feeling that the farmer might have some cunning trick up his sleeve. Captain hadn't changed his mind. He still didn't believe in magic. No, siree. But there was something unreal about that llama, something *unnatural*. Was it possible that the animal could multiply itself? That it could be in two, or three, or even *four* places at the same time?

Captain shook away the thought. Good heavens! If that were possible, why, coyotes might never eat lamb again! It was a ridiculous idea and Captain was glad he hadn't spoken of it aloud. If word got out, other coyotes would think he was crazy, losing his marbles.

No, he'd never consider it again.

Tonight they'd get what they'd come for if it were the last thing he ever did.

So as soon as it was fully dark, Captain Coyote and Cupcake set off through the woods towards the farm, for their final showdown with Lewie.

Chapter Eight

The Show Must Go On

The sun was beginning to go down on a successful day of rehearsals.

Lewie and the flock were almost ready for their big performance. They were waiting until the end of the day to be sure there'd be no more visits from the farmer, to avoid the disappointment of being interrupted in mid-song or dance.

All the sheep and lambs gathered round for Lewie's final encouraging words. He'd prepared a strong, rallying speech. But when he looked at their excited faces, he knew that wasn't necessary. Instead, he beamed at everyone and told them, "I am so proud of you." The sheep blinked – and blushed. "I know everyone's going to give it one hundred and ten per cent."

"…and ten per cent," the sheep chorused.

"I just have one regret," Lewie finished, "and that is that you won't have an audience to watch your wonderful show."

The sheep shrugged. An audience would

have been nice, but they'd already had so much fun. And they would watch each other and cheer each other on.

Lewie had given everyone helpful notes and now there was little left to say. They only needed to wait for the moon to provide a spotlight for them to perform in.

The sheep were doing their own final practice, as well as dealing with their lambs' last-minute nerves. It wasn't ideal putting on the show so late, past their bedtime, but excitement was keeping them all awake.

Then suddenly, out of the woods, came a chilling sound. A sharp chorus of howling that made every animal stop and freeze on the spot. Lewie knew exactly what it was and so did the sheep, but the lambs were too young ever to have heard the heart-stopping warning call of coyotes.

"What was that?" they asked their mothers. The sheep looked to Lewie before they answered. He knew this was the moment it'd all been leading up to, when he would have to take charge.

Lewie knew how he *should* be feeling and acting – like a strong, brave and reassuring Guard Llama. But he felt only one thing – *panic*. His knees were knocking together, his mouth was dry, his heart was racing. His ears lay back and a groaning noise – *mwaaa* – was rising in his throat. He couldn't take care of all these sheep and their lambs. He wanted to run away and hide.

"This is ridiculous," Lewie told himself.
"What am I doing here, pretending to be a
Guard Llama? I can't fight coyotes. I hate
fighting! My brothers were right, I'm just
a joke. Making animals laugh is all I'm
good for."

Lewie looked down at the trusting faces, all depending on him. The sheep, who knew what danger was, and the little lambs that hadn't yet learnt about it. Then Lewie remembered the words of his twin sister, Liberty. *Just stick to what you're good at, and believe in yourself.*

Danger might be on its way, but it wasn't here yet. The most important thing right now, Lewie realised, was that they should carry on with the show. It would calm the sheep and maybe give him the confidence he needed.

It was a risk, he knew that. If the sheep decided he was crazy and chose to run away, there'd be a huge stampede. It would all end in chaos and disaster. But it was a risk worth taking.

"Well, what are we waiting for?" Lewie asked in his most confident voice. "Let's get this show on the road!"

Captain Coyote and Cupcake came out of the trees very close to the fence. They'd sent a clear warning and now they were ready to attack.

Captain had been talking tactics to Cupcake.

"The purpose of the threatening call," he explained, "is to send the flock into panic. The sheep will scatter and the Guard Llama will be so busy trying to round them all up and keep them calm he won't be ready to face our attack when it comes. We'll be in there really fast, pick up as many lambs as we can carry, and out again before you can say Captain Cornelius Coyote. Are you ready, my boy, because this will be a night to remember," he promised Cupcake.

And it was a night to remember, but not in the way Captain expected.

Instead of a flock of sheep in chaos, the coyotes found a small group of lambs standing in the spotlight, sweetly singing:

"Home, home on the range,
Where the deer and the antelope play,
Where seldom is heard a discouraging word
And the skies are not cloudy all day…"

Captain could barely believe his eyes –
or his ears. Were these sheep completely
fearless – or plain crazy?

Cupcake was already dazzled. The young
coyote dropped to the ground, wriggling
forward for a better view. Captain had
no choice but to join him. They watched
the entire show, as sheep and lambs sang,
danced and performed a huge
variety of tricks. Cupcake's
favourite part was when
one group after another
of nervous little lambs
did gymnastics, tap
dancing, hip-hop –
even body popping.

"This is *sooooo* cool," he told his uncle. Captain rolled his eyes.

There were acts that made the whole audience laugh and one or two that almost made them cry. Because, to Lewie's delight, there was an audience after all.

Word had somehow got round the farm, and any animals and all the poultry that were free to roam, had turned up to watch the show.

Even Millie was there. All day she'd known something special was happening and she was determined not to miss it. Without a word to her mum and dad, she'd slipped out of bed. In her nightdress and wellingtons, she'd made her way down to the field. Following her as usual were her puppy and her duck. Altogether there was a good-sized audience.

Even the llamas, in their enclosure, were craning their necks to see what was going on. Mama and Papa Llama couldn't understand what Lewie was thinking of. Everyone had heard the coyotes' call. The whole herd had come to alert, knowing an attack was about to happen. They'd all waited to see what Lewie would do. This was not at all what they'd expected.

How could he just ignore it and carry on with his drama nonsense? That's what Papa Llama wanted to know. He called out to Lewie, braying at the top of his voice, trying to bring the boy to his senses. But his voice was drowned out by the performing sheep.

Mama Llama was anxious too, but she couldn't help being impressed with what Lewie had created. She was so proud of him. In her heart of hearts she felt sure Lewie would triumph – somehow!

The show was finally drawing to a close. Captain Coyote had found himself almost as dazzled as his nephew. But when it was over he gave himself a good shaking. He was older and wiser than Cupcake and should have known better. This wasn't what they'd come here for – watching animals do tricks. They had a job to do and now was the time to do it. The evidence was before his eyes – there was only *one* Guard Llama. The sheep would run at the first sight of him and Cupcake, and the llama would probably run too. This was going to be *so* easy.

"OK, let's go," Captain whispered to Cupcake. "Keep close behind me."

He moved forward, preparing to attack.

When the show finished there was a deafening chorus of stamping and bleating and clapping and crowing and cheering that went on and on.

Lewie finally stepped forward to speak.

But before he could say a word he was faced with the chilling sight of a large coyote creeping relentlessly towards him.

Behind the large coyote was a smaller one, but what Lewie couldn't know was how many more there might be hiding in the shadows. Maybe a whole pack of them. Still he didn't hesitate.

"Everyone fall in behind me. Quickly!" he ordered.

On his command, the sheep closed ranks and formed a huge body of animals, shaking but united behind their leader. The mothers tucked the lambs safely between their legs and waited for Lewie's instructions.

They weren't brave; they were sheep,

after all. But they were ready to fight behind him to protect their lambs if they had to.

Captain Coyote and Lewie eyed each other. They waited to see who would make the first move. Lewie had no idea how strong – or weak – or brave – he might be, but any moment now he was going to find out.

Captain crept forward, step by step, his belly close to the ground. Lewie lowered his head and stamped hard, drumming the ground with his feet. It was a warning and it took Captain by surprise. He'd expected the llama to run at the first sight of him. He hesitated, but only for a split second, then advanced again. Lewie continued to stamp his feet aggressively, braying loudly to warn the coyote off.

"Keep away from *my* flock," he was saying loud and clear.

But Captain wasn't that easily scared off. He bared his teeth and continued to move forward.

One or two of the lambs were so terrified, they'd got separated from their mothers. Out of the corner of his eye Lewie spotted two now – Shoo and Bertie. And so did Captain.

The old coyote could see he'd possibly underestimated this

llama, but he wasn't going away tonight with empty paws. No, siree. He made a lightning dash to the side, almost snatching the lambs up in his jaws. But somehow Lewie was there before him. He set himself between the coyote and the lambs. He reared up, kicking and spitting and braying.

He was defending his flock with a passion he had no idea he possessed. Lewie didn't care what happened to him, but he would *not* let those coyotes touch his sheep.

Captain retreated, but he wasn't finished yet, not by a long way. He'd take a little time to re-think then he'd make another attack. And keep on attacking. This llama was young and inexperienced. It might take a little longer, but in the end Captain would win because he would not give up.

One thing he'd tried to impress upon Cupcake was always to ensure that your getaway route was clear. Captain turned briefly to check it now. Suddenly, he stopped and froze. He had no idea how it was possible, but there was the evidence before his eyes. Another llama.

Captain looked back at the sheep enclosure. The young Guard Llama was still standing there, protecting them. So how could he be here as well, *behind the coyotes*, ready to cut off their retreat?

It was too creepy! Captain's head snapped back and forth. There could be no denying it. Two identical llamas – one in front of him and one behind. And who knew how many more waiting in the shadows? Any second he and Cupcake could be surrounded with no way to escape!

Captain's old heart began to pound with fear. He remembered one of the first rules he'd ever taught his nephew. *He who retreats, lives to hunt another day.*

He opened his jaws and gave Cupcake a shrill warning bark. Then the pair of them went yelping and howling, zigzagging back through the woods. Captain ran as fast as his old legs would carry him, aware that he was definitely getting too old for this game.

Chapter Nine

The End of the Show

Still in the sheep enclosure, Lewie was surprised to hear the cries of the coyotes disappearing into the distance. He hadn't expected them to give up so easily. But before he and the flock had time to celebrate, another surprise emerged from the shadows. Farmer Palmer and his wife had come in search of their missing daughter.

Millie's mother had looked in on her during the evening, only to find an empty bed. It hadn't taken them long to guess where they might find the little girl.

As they set off, the farmer had heard the unmistakable sound of coyotes, so he was carrying his gun just in case. But he really didn't need it. Lewie had everything under control. Farmer Palmer and his wife arrived just in time to see the llama drive off two coyotes, one at least full-grown. *What a brave and powerful fight Lewie put up,* thought the farmer.

"Thank goodness I listened to Millie," he told his wife. "She said all along that Lewie was a llama in a million. And she was right."

Farmer Palmer gave Lewie a big hug and plenty more praise, while the flock of sheep stood by watching, sharing Lewie's pride.

"That's what I always said," Ginger whispered to her friends. "A *llama in a million*."

"…in a million," her friends echoed.

The farmer picked up his sleepy daughter and turned for home.

"If I hadn't seen it with my own eyes," he told his wife, "I never would have believed it. What an animal! Strong, brave, fearless, yet gentle and reliable. And such a character…"

All the way back to the farmhouse the farmer went on listing Lewie's qualities. At the same time, a sleepy Millie kept trying to tell her parents a very strange mixed-up tale about tap-dancing sheep and acrobatic lambs…

Her father kissed her fondly on the head. He wished he was only six years old again and dreaming up such fantastic stories.

After the farmer had left, Lewie tried to encourage the sheep to get their lambs off to bed.

"That's enough about me," he told them. "Some of these lambs are falling asleep on their feet."

But the sheep kept on hanging around, sharing their own particular highlights from the show.

"I liked your bit best," Shirley told Shelley.

"…your bit best," Shelley repeated.

"…*your* bit best," Sheila insisted.

"It was *all* brilliant," Ginger announced. "The best night of my life."

"…of my life," all the other sheep agreed.

"Who's the greatest?" Bertie bleated.

"Lewie's the greatest!" Shoo answered.

All the lambs joined in, and then all the sheep took up the cry too. "Who's the greatest? Lewie's the greatest!"

It rippled across the field while Lewie was still busy helping to collect up odd lambs that were dotted about, curled up like little woolly balls. As he listened, his chest swelled with pride.

As the mother sheep went off to bed they

were still telling each other they'd never been happier. But, more importantly, they'd never felt safer.

"Look how scary Lewie was, when he needed to be," bleated Shona.

"Yet he's so good with the lambs," bleated Shula.

"Much better than that *Terminator*," added Ginger, trying to have the last bleat as usual. "Haven't I always said so?"

But Sheila summed it up for everyone. "He's the ideal Guard Llama," she bleated.

"...Guard Llama," they all bleated together.

By now, the coyotes were back in their

burrow. Captain was still trying to make sense of what had just happened. After all the excitement, Cupcake had fallen into a deep sleep. The old coyote looked at him tenderly. If anything had happened to his young nephew he would never have forgiven himself.

Tomorrow he would take him home to his family. And Captain would pass on the word, tell every coyote for miles – keep well away from Farmer Palmer's farm. But he'd keep his suspicions about supernatural llamas with special powers to himself. He didn't want other coyotes thinking he was going crazy. No, siree! Maybe one day, though, in the future, he'd come back here and get to the bottom of it all.

Just then Cupcake woke briefly, maybe from a bad dream. He asked to be told yet again about the taste of tender, young, spring lamb.

But Captain said, "Forget about lamb, my boy. There's other things just as good as lamb, you know. There's rabbits; how about we catch one of those tomorrow? Then there's lizard – *de-licious*. And fish. Mmm, mmm. And don't forget frogs! Have I ever told you what a great delicacy frogs are?"

Lewie couldn't go to sleep before talking to his family. Now that he'd finally proved himself, surely that would be OK. And of course it was. Everyone was there, waiting at the fence to congratulate him.

"We're so proud of you," Mama and Papa Lama called to him.

"I know I had my doubts," Papa Llama admitted, "but I'm pleased to say you proved me wrong, son. You were every bit as good as *The Terminator*."

This was high praise indeed and Mama Llama was as pleased to hear it as Lewie was.

Even Lewie's older brothers congratulated him. Although, quietly, they agreed it wasn't the way they'd have handled it. But, still, Lewie had done… OK.

Latisha shook her head, tutting as usual. But she also managed to admit, "You done good, Lewie. Better than these two idiots would've, that's for sure. Tchhh."

Lewie's younger brothers and sisters wanted to know, "Weren't you afraid, though, Lewie? We would have been."

"There wasn't time to be afraid," Lewie told them. "It all happened so fast. Anyway, you just do what you've got to do, to look after your flock." It made Lewie blush a bit to say those words out loud.

"Yeah, but… being all on your own?" they persisted.

"I wasn't on my own," Lewie told them. "I had all the sheep behind me."

The llamas thought this was one of Lewie's best jokes ever. They shook with laughter. "Sheep behind him," Leo and Lamar snorted as if Lewie had told them he'd faced the coyotes with a swarm of butterflies backing him up.

But Lewie hadn't been joking. He had

felt supported, knowing all the sheep were there, willing him on. They probably couldn't have done much, but still they were there, behind him.

Lewie peered into the dark, but he couldn't see the person he really wanted to talk to.

"Where's Liberty?" he finally asked.

Mama and Papa Llama shook their heads.

"I do despair of that girl," Papa Llama said.

"She's got out again," Mama Llama said anxiously.

"Tchhh! No one's seen her all night," Latisha told him.

"One of these days she might not come back," sobbed Mama Llama.

"She'll come back," Lewie said reassuringly. "She always does."

It was very late by this time and everyone was sleepy. The llamas began to drift away. Lewie was tired too, but he felt he ought to do a final round of the field. As he started out he heard a voice nearby whisper, "Hey, over here, Lew."

In the darkness, coming out of the woods, Lewie could just make out the shape of his sister, Liberty. He was so glad to see her, not least to know she was safe.

"How did you get out this time?" Lewie asked.

182

Liberty grinned. "You know they haven't built the fence yet that could keep me in," she said. "Oh, Lew, you were brilliant. That was some show you put on."

Lewie bobbed his head and sighed. It still felt a bit unreal to him.

"I was surprised they gave up so easily," he admitted. "I thought that big one would be back."

"Oh, you scared him off," she said proudly. "With his tail between his legs. And that little one was barely old enough to be out at night."

"Did you see them, then?" Lewie asked, surprised.

"Oh, just from a distance," Liberty

said lightly.

"Well, something must have scared them off," said Lewie.

"*You* scared them off," Liberty said. Lewie didn't need to know the whole truth.

"But what would I have done if there'd been more of them?" Lewie asked, suddenly full of self-doubt.

"You'd have handled it," his sister told him. "Just like you did this time – *all on your own*. You were wonderful."

Lewie smiled and thought how lucky he was to have people who had such confidence in him.

"Better get back," said Liberty, "before Mama and Papa have a fit. I'll come and see you again soon," she promised.

As Lewie watched his sister trotting home he suddenly felt a couple of little lambs tugging on his tail.

"Lewie. Lewie, we can't sleep. Will you tell us a story?"

"It's far too late for a story," Lewie told them. But he nudged the lambs back to their mothers and then finally settled them down with a couple of rounds of 'Baa, Baa, Black Sheep'.

Across the farm all was finally quiet and peaceful. In the farmhouse, Farmer Palmer slept easy, knowing that his prize-winning sheep were completely safe. His daughter,

Millie, was remembering the most exciting day of her little life so far. In her dreams, she found she could talk to the animals and understand everything they said to her.

All the sheep and lambs were asleep and dreaming too. Some were reliving their moments in the spotlight; some were basking in their children's glory. Others were just happy to have been there and seen it all. And in their dreams, yet more were having their own thrilling adventures, single-handedly beating off attacks from whole packs of wild creatures.

But after all the evening's drama, there was one animal that was still awake – or maybe half asleep. Lewie, with one eye

open, was still looking out for his flock.

"Goodnight, Lewie," he told himself, yawning. "Sleep tight. Don't let the coyotes bite."

Llama Drama

Going for Gold!

Farmer Palmer enters Lewie and his herd of lambs
in the agility contest at the County Fair. They
train hard and get through the first round but then
disaster strikes – the lambs mysteriously go missing!
Someone is trying to cheat . . . Lewie must put
his bravery to the test and search for the lambs.
Will he find them in time to go for gold?

Coming in August 2013

Awesome Animals

Awesome adventures with the wildest wildlife!

Meerkat Madness
IAN WHYBROW

MERRY Meerkat Madness
IAN WHYBROW

Meerkat Madness
IAN WHYBROW

More Meerkat Madness
IAN WHYBROW

Meerkat Madness Flying High
Wup, wup and away!
IAN WHYBROW

Watch out for the world's wildest pandas!
PANDA PANIC
Jamie Rix

PANDA PANIC RUNNING WILD
Jamie Rix

Penguin Pandemonium
Little birds, big dreams
Jeanne Willis

Penguin Pandemonium
THE RESCUE

Coming in 2013!

PENGUIN PANDEMONUIM – THE WILD BEAST

KOALA CALAMITY – SURF'S UP!

OTTER CHAOS – THE DAM BUSTERS

LLAMA DRAMA – GOING FOR GOLD!

PENGUIN PANDEMONIUM – CHRISTMAS CRACKERS